THE LITTLE
DRUMMER BOY

Louis Weber, C.E.O.
Publications International, Ltd.
7373 North Cicero Avenue
Lincolnwood, Illinois 60646

Permission is never granted for commercial purposes.

Manufactured in USA.

8   7   6   5   4   3   2   1

ISBN 1-56173-714-3

Contributing writer: Carolyn Quattrocki

Cover illustration: Linda Graves

Book illustrations: Susan Spellman

Publications International, Ltd.

A long time ago, near the town of Bethlehem, lived a little boy. His family was very poor. His clothes were not fancy. Sometimes he was hungry, because there was not enough food to eat.

But the boy had one thing that made his life happy. The little boy had a drum. The drum had belonged to his father, and before that, to his grandfather. Years before, when his grandfather was young, a group of traveling musicians had come to the little village. His grandfather was given the drum by the musicians.

When the little boy was old enough, they taught him to play *pa-rum pum pum pum*. Now the drum belonged to him.

The little boy loved his drum more than anything in the world. In fact, he played his drum every day all around his village. The other children in the village would follow behind him, marching and singing along as he played. Sometimes, even the animals joined the parade!

The boy played his drum so often and so well that the people in the village began to call him Little Drummer Boy. They always smiled as they heard him playing and singing:

Pa-rum pum pum pum,
Me and my drum.

At the same time, in a town called Nazareth, there lived a young girl named Mary. One day, the Angel Gabriel appeared to Mary and told her that she would have a son and should name the baby Jesus.

Now, Caesar Augustus, who was the ruler of the land, sent out an order. All the people had to go to the town where they were born. There, the tax collectors would count them and write down their names.

So Mary and her husband, Joseph, set out on the long journey from Nazareth to Bethlehem. They had to travel slowly, because Mary was expecting a baby. Mary rode on a donkey, and Joseph walked along beside her.

When Mary and Joseph finally arrived in Bethlehem, it was crowded with all the people who had come to be counted. Joseph asked at many houses for a place to spend the night, but no one had room for them. Night was coming, and it was growing cold outside.

Finally, Joseph and Mary came to an inn. They again asked for a room. The innkeeper said, "I have no room inside, but there is a stable behind the inn where you could stay with the animals overnight."

Mary and Joseph were so cold and tired they were happy to have any place to spend the night. So they went to the little stable and slept on the hay beside the animals.

During the night, the baby was born. It was a boy, just as the Angel Gabriel had said. Mary named the baby Jesus and wrapped him up in warm clothes. She made a bed for him by putting hay in a manger. Then she carefully laid him down on the hay.

That same night, some shepherds nearby were out in the field watching over their sheep. All of a sudden, an angel appeared to them and told them about the birth of the baby Jesus.

The angel said, "Go to Bethlehem, where you will find the newborn baby, lying in a manger." Then many angels appeared and sang, "Peace on earth and good will to all." When the angels disappeared, the shepherds hurried to where the baby Jesus lay.

Everyone was talking about baby Jesus and wanted to take gifts to him. The Little Drummer Boy heard this and thought, "I want to go to see Jesus, too. But what can I take as a present?"

That night, when he started to Bethlehem, he saw a magnificent sight. In front of him were three kings, their camels laden with heavy saddlebags. The kings were dressed in the finest clothes the boy had ever seen. Were they also going to see the baby Jesus?

The Little Drummer Boy listened as he followed them. "There is the star we follow," said one. "That bright and shining star has led us over many lands for many nights. See, it points us toward the stable up ahead."

The three kings followed the star to the manger where the baby Jesus lay. When the kings arrived there, all the people who had gathered around stood back. "Who are you?" asked a shepherd.

"My name is Melchior," said the first. "I have brought a gift of gold for the newborn baby." The second said, "I am Gaspar. I have brought frankincense, a rare and beautiful perfume." "And my name is Balthazar," said the third. "I, too, have brought a valuable perfume, called myrrh."

The three kings laid their gifts before the manger and said, "We have followed the star for many miles to see the newborn baby."

The Little Drummer Boy saw the beautiful gifts the kings had brought. He thought, "Oh, what can I do? I have nothing to give!" Turning to leave, he hung his head and began to walk away.

Then he saw the drum at his side. Suddenly he knew what his gift could be. He would sing and play his drum for the baby Jesus! He started singing softly at the edge of the crowd:

Come they told me, pa-rum pum pum pum,
Our newborn King to see, pa-rum pum pum pum,
Our finest gifts to bring, pa-rum pum pum pum
To lay before the King, pa-rum pum pum pum
*   Rum pum pum pum, rum pum pum pum,*
So to honor Him, pa-rum pum pum pum,
When we come.

When the Drummer Boy began to play and sing, the crowd parted to let him through. As he came nearer the manger, he sang:

Baby Jesus, pa-rum pum pum pum,
I am a poor boy, too, pa-rum pum pum pum,
I have no gift to bring, pa-rum pum pum pum,
That's fit to give a king, pa-rum pum pum pum,
  Rum pum pum pum, rum pum pum pum,
Shall I play for you, pa-rum pum pum pum,
On my drum?

Mary knew that the poor boy was giving the best gift he had—the gift of love. She smiled and nodded her head for him to finish:

Mary nodded, pa-rum pum pum pum,
The ox and lamb kept time,
  pa-rum pum pum pum,

I played my drum for Him,
  pa-rum pum pum pum,
I played my best for him, pa-rum pum pum pum,
  Rum pum pum pum, rum pum pum pum
Then He smiled at me, pa-rum pum pum pum
Me and my drum.